CRICKET HELPS OUT
Understanding Appendicitis

By **PAT McCAW, M.D.**
Illustrated by **BETH HUGHES**

MAYO CLINIC PRESS KIDS

With gratitude to the Mayo Clinic Child Life Services Team

© 2024 Mayo Foundation for Medical Education and Research. All rights reserved. MAYO, MAYO CLINIC and the triple-shield Mayo logo are trademarks and service marks of MFMER.

MAYO CLINIC PRESS KIDS | An imprint of Mayo Clinic Press
200 First St. SW
Rochester, MN 55905
mcpress.mayoclinic.org
To stay informed about Mayo Clinic Press, please subscribe to our free e-newsletter at mcpress.mayoclinic.org or follow us on social media.

Published in the United States by Mayo Clinic Press Kids, an imprint of Mayo Clinic Press. All rights reserved. No part of this publication may be reproduced, stored in a retrieval system, or transmitted, in any form or by any means, electronic, mechanical, photocopying, recording, or otherwise, without the prior written permission of the publisher.

The medical information in this book is true and complete to the best of our knowledge. This book is intended as an informative guide for those wishing to learn more about health issues. It is not intended to replace, countermand or conflict with advice given to you by your own physician. The ultimate decision concerning your care should be made between you and your doctor. Information in this book is offered with no guarantees. The author and publisher disclaim all liability in connection with the use of this book. The views expressed are the author's personal views, and do not necessarily reflect the policy or position of Mayo Clinic.

For bulk sales to employers, member groups, and health-related companies, contact Mayo Clinic at SpecialSalesMayoBooks@mayo.edu.

Proceeds from the sale of every book benefit important medical research and education at Mayo Clinic.

ISBN: 978-1-945564-98-7 (paperback) | 978-1-945564-99-4 (library binding) | 978-0-9627865-3-2 (ebook) | 979-8-88770-094-6 (multiuser PDF) | 979-8-88770-093-9 (multiuser ePub)

Library of Congress Control Number: 2023001111. Library of Congress Cataloging-in-Publication Data is available upon request.

TABLE OF CONTENTS

CHAPTER 1: MEET CRICKET 4

CHAPTER 2: HOSPITAL HELPERS 12

CHAPTER 3: MADDIE'S BELLY 20

CHAPTER 4: STARTING AN IV 32

CHAPTER 5: SAM NEEDS A SCAN 42

CHAPTER 6: REST & RECOVERY 58

CHAPTER 7: THE LUCKIEST PUP 70

More about Appendicitis 74
More about Facility Dogs 76
Meet Alicia! 78

MEET CRICKET

THE WARM WATER FROM THE NOZZLE SOAKS MY FUR, weighing me down. I scoot over to the corner of the tub to dodge the spray.

"You're so squirmy, Cricket!" Tunde's deep laugh bounces off the bathroom walls. "I know you don't like bath time, but tomorrow we go to the hospital."

Tunde picks me up and places me back under the spraying water. *Ugh.*

Tunde is my handler. Even though he makes me take a bath, he's still the greatest human. He whistles throughout the house, and his laugh is contagious. If only he could put up with my doggy smell.

Then it hits me. Tunde said we're going back to work tomorrow! My ears perk up as water drips off my face. We get to go help kids in the hospital. My wagging tail sends water flying all over Tunde.

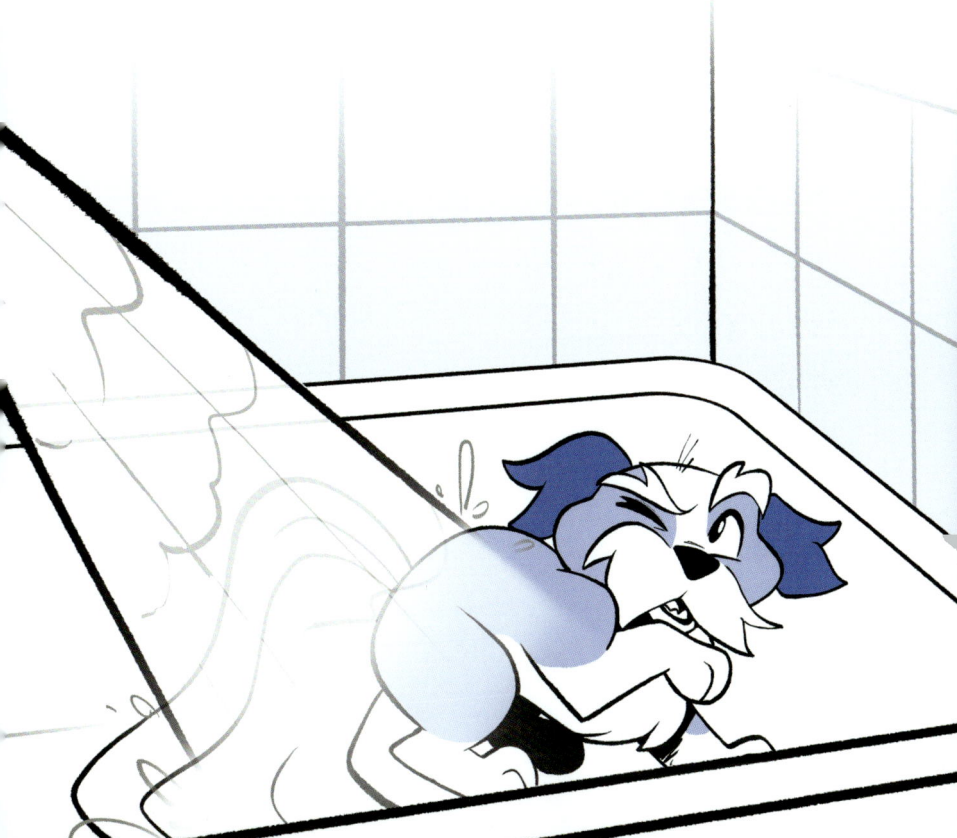

Tunde chuckles as he shields himself from the spray. "You're a good girl, Cricket. Tomorrow will be a busy day. Are you ready?"

Are you kidding? I can't wait! I lick Tunde's arm.

Tunde wipes his face, and his laughter fills the room. "I'm excited, too! Now, who's going to clean up this mess?"

Tunde is a Certified Child Life Specialist (CCLS). I've lived with him for the last two months since I graduated from Helping Paws Academy. I'm a certified facility dog, and I'm so lucky to have Tunde. He and I cruise the hospital helping kids understand their illnesses and recover from procedures.

Tunde dries off my long hair, and I give a wiggle and shake. I look like a mop, but I sure do smell clean.

Tunde puts on his dog bone pajamas, hops into bed, and leans over to scratch my ears. "Get some rest tonight, Cricket."

I snuggle into my fluffy bed on the floor and nuzzle Ralph, my moose. One of his antlers droops from so much love, but he still makes me happy. My eyes grow heavy, and I drift off to sleep. In my dream, the kids at the hospital cheer me on as I leap to catch a Frisbee.

The following day, the sunlight warms my nose. Tunde has already showered and clipped his hospital ID badge to his shirt.

I stretch and yawn. After tucking Ralph into my dog bed, I run to Tunde.

"Are you ready, girl? Let's get you walked and fed before we head to work."

My whole body wiggles as my tail wags. We go out for a quick walk around the block before I chow down on my kibble. Then we're ready for work. Tunde fits me into my Helping Paws uniform and attaches my leash. I'm looking good!

I used to get nervous when I saw the blue vest, but not anymore. Seeing the kids makes me happy, and their smiles make me want to dance. I'm the luckiest dog ever.

HOSPITAL HELPERS

MY PAWS BOUNCE OFF THE SIDEWALK AS WE APPROACH the hospital. Inside the building, the overhead light fixtures catch the sunlight and create rainbows on the walls. Everything smells clean and fresh—like me! Staff walk around in white coats or scrubs. Patients, doctors, nurses, and custodians say hello to Tunde, and I get lots of head scratches.

"Good morning, Cricket!" Sandy sits behind the reception desk. She rubs behind my right shoulder, and I lean into her arm. Sandy knows it's my secret scratching spot. I stick out my tongue with a happy pant.

Tunde stops at the desk to print off a list of patients for the day. As I wait, I see my friends Lumos and Dash walk by with their handlers.

Dash and I met at Helping Paws Academy. And Lumos has worked at the hospital with his handler, Eun Ji, for more than two years! Lumos nods to me. "Good morning, Cricket. Let's put in an excellent day for the kids!"

My cheeks get warm, and my stomach does a flip. Lumos stands tall, strong, and cool. I still feel a little nervous when I'm around him.

"You'll do great, Cricket," Lumos says as he and Eun Ji walk off. "I'm on my way to help Thomas put a puzzle together in physical therapy!"

Dash's handler, Navya, is also a CCLS. She steps up next to Tunde to print out her patient list. "Good morning, Tunde. Are you and Cricket ready for a big day?"

I wag my tail, and Tunde nods his head toward me. "Cricket says we're ready!"

I poke Dash's shoulder and whisper, "I hope someone wants to nap today. Last week, I fetched the ball twenty times with Lee in neurology. He wore me out!"

"Playing ball sounds fun!" Dash says. "Yesterday, I walked with a little girl and then caught the Frisbee. I didn't think being a facility dog could be so exciting!"

It's Dash's first month on the job. She was nervous at first but caught on fast.

I nod in agreement. "Every day is a new adventure. I'm dragging my tail a bit today, but I know I'll perk up as soon as I see our first patient. Have a good day, Dash."

Tunde tugs on my leash and leads us to our first patient. "Come, Cricket. Let's get to work."

I say goodbye to Dash and keep pace with Tunde's stride. As we wait for the elevator, a nurse approaches. I recognize Rita from previous emergency room visits.

"Good morning, Tunde. I know you and Cricket are in high demand, but we could use your help in the emergency room." Rita scratches my ears. "Cricket, a nine-year-old patient named Maddie has

appendicitis. She's feeling scared—I'm hoping you and Tunde can visit her."

Tunde folds up his patient list and places it in his pocket. "We're always ready to help."

Rita clasps her hands together and bounces on her toes. "Great! You both can help Maddie learn what's going to happen next. Maybe you can even make her smile."

I heel at Tunde's side as we hurry to the ER. I wish I could charge ahead! I'm determined to find Maddie's smile.

MADDIE'S BELLY

THE ER BUZZES WITH DOCTORS AND NURSES. Staff hurry from room to room, and I hear a baby cry down the hall. The double doors fly open. People in blue uniforms hurry past, pushing a patient on a long bed. Multiple bandages cover the patient's leg. My heart races. Will I be up to the task of helping Maddie?

Tunde notices my hesitation and gently tugs on the leash. "It's okay, Cricket. You've got this."

I take a deep breath. *This is what I've trained for.* I hop back in stride next to Tunde. He always reminds me that we're here to help.

Rita leads us toward a room, and I hear soft voices coming from inside. As we get closer, I see a young girl lying on her side in the bed, a stuffed rabbit by her cheek. The girl is curled into a ball, holding her belly. She whimpers, and her cheeks are flushed.

"It hurts, Mommy." She looks up to her mother, whose face wrinkles with worry.

"I know it hurts, Maddie. We're here to get you better." Maddie's mom squeezes her daughter's hand and strokes her hair.

A tear falls down Maddie's cheek. "I want to go home."

Tunde and I walk into the room, and Rita introduces us to Maddie and her parents, Mr. and Mrs. Tan. "Tunde is a Certified Child Life Specialist, and this is his friend Cricket."

I step forward, and Maddie's eyes grow big. "A dog!" she whispers.

"Maddie, is it okay if Cricket sits beside you on your bed?" Tunde asks. Maddie nods. The bed is too high for me to jump, so Tunde gives me a lift.

I ease onto Maddie's bed and curl up next to her. Her body radiates heat, like I'm sitting next to a fireplace. She breathes

fast, and her eyes look glassy. She reaches her arm up and runs a weak hand down my back. Her voice is quiet. "Hi, Cricket. You're cute."

Suddenly, Maddie squeezes her eyes closed and grabs her belly. "Mom, it hurts!"

I lay my head on Maddie's arm. I wish I could make her pain go away!

Tunde pulls a chair up to Maddie's bed and speaks calmly. "Maddie, I'm sorry it hurts. The doctors and nurses are here to help you feel better. And my job is to help answer your questions. Do you know what the appendix is?"

Maddie nods weakly and points to her lower belly. "It's here."

Tunde nods. "Yes. The appendix is a small pocket on the colon. Sometimes, it becomes infected. When that happens, it can cause tummy pain, swelling, and a fever."

Maddie whimpers and says, "I was up all night with pain in my belly. It hurts right here." She points to her right side.

"She spiked a 102 fever this morning," Mr. Tan adds.

That explains why Maddie's body feels so hot under my chin!

Tunde nods and looks at Maddie. "I know the doctors have told you the best thing to help your body right now is surgery. A surgeon is a specialized doctor who can remove your appendix so you start to feel better."

Maddie shakes, and her tears soak the fur on my ear. I reach my paw out and rest it on her arm. I want her to know that I'm here for her. Maddie pulls me closer to her cheek as she cries.

"One important thing to know," Tunde continues, "is that your appendix doesn't have a job inside your body. So your body won't even notice when it's gone. And because your appendix is infected, your body will feel much better once it's removed."

"Will it hurt?" Maddie asks.

Tunde shakes his head and explains that Maddie will be asleep during the entire surgery.

"The doctors will give you a medicine called anesthesia. This medicine makes sure you're asleep and don't feel anything. After the surgery is all done, you'll wake up."

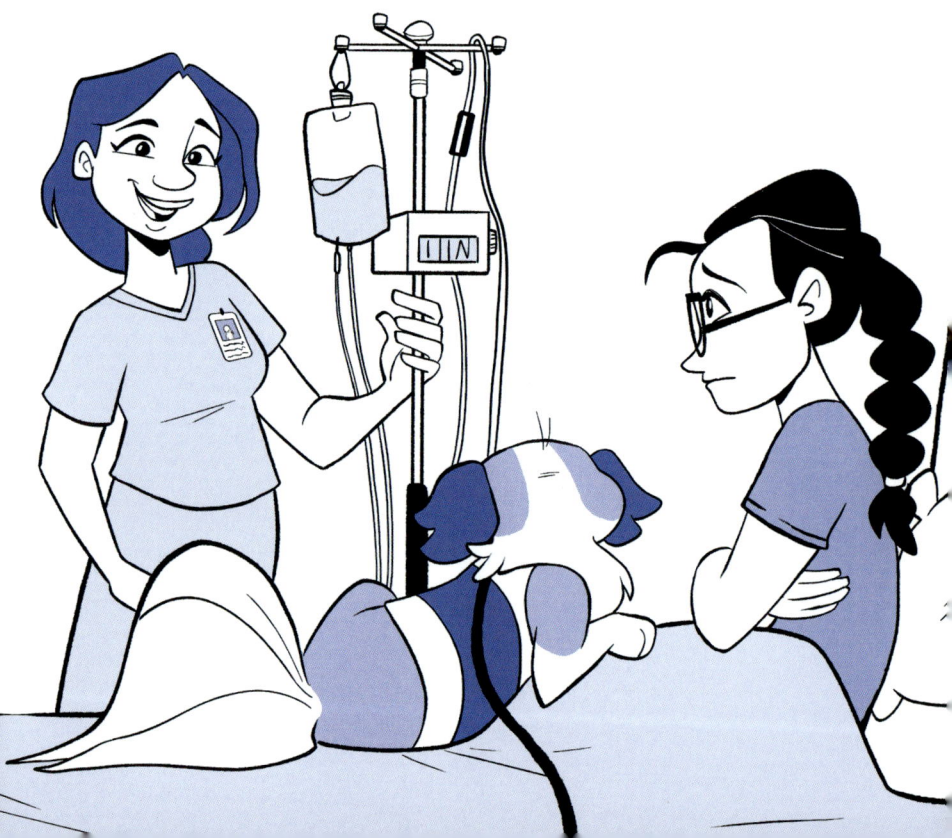

Maddie squeezes my neck but doesn't say anything. I stay still and keep snuggling.

Rita returns to the room with a handful of supplies. "Maddie, we need to put in an IV before they take you to surgery."

Maddie stiffens. "What's that mean?"

Tunde's voice is calm. "It's okay to feel nervous, Maddie. Cricket and I can help you learn all about what to expect."

Rita prepares the IV supplies at Maddie's bedside. I stay close to Maddie as more tears fall.

STARTING AN IV

RITA EXPLAINS THAT AN IV IS A TINY TUBE THAT HELPS fluids and medicines get into the body. "There'll be a small poke to get the IV into your arm," Rita says, "but we can use some cold spray or numbing cream to help with the pain."

Maddie holds her arm tight against her chest. "I don't want a needle in my arm."

"I wouldn't either, Maddie," Tunde says. "The good news is the needle doesn't stay in your arm. It helps get the tube into the right spot, but then it's removed. Meanwhile, the flexible IV stays inside your vein to give you medicine."

I want to help Maddie relax. Her body is tense, and I can feel her trembling. Her belly hurts, and she has to get her arm poked. I look at Tunde with big eyes.

"Maddie, I have an idea. It's scary when you don't know what to expect. What if we pretend to demonstrate an IV on Cricket?"

Maddie's eyebrows rise, but she doesn't say anything.

"We'll be right back," Tunde says with a smile. He and I go get his backpack. When we return, Tunde opens the backpack wide so I can see what's inside. He looks at me and commands, "Get."

I know exactly what to do! I nose my way into Tunde's backpack and pull out our toy medical kit. *What a great idea!*

Mr. Tan leans forward and rests his hand on Maddie's shoulder. "Look at that, Maddie. Cricket's going to show you how you'll get an IV."

I follow Tunde's lead. He opens the play medical kit and pulls out a toy syringe. He points it at my foot. "You will feel a slight poke as the needle enters the skin. I'm going to count to three so Cricket knows when the small poke will happen. And Cricket will hold her paw very still so I can get the IV in just the right spot."

I hold my paw very still as Tunde demonstrates.

"The needle places a small tube called a catheter inside your vein. After the poke, the needle is removed while the catheter stays inside." Tunde holds up a sample IV catheter to show Maddie. "Feel the plastic? No poking points."

Maddie leans forward and touches the end of the catheter. "It bends like a straw."

"Exactly," Tunde says. "The catheter stays in your arm during surgery so they can give you medicine."

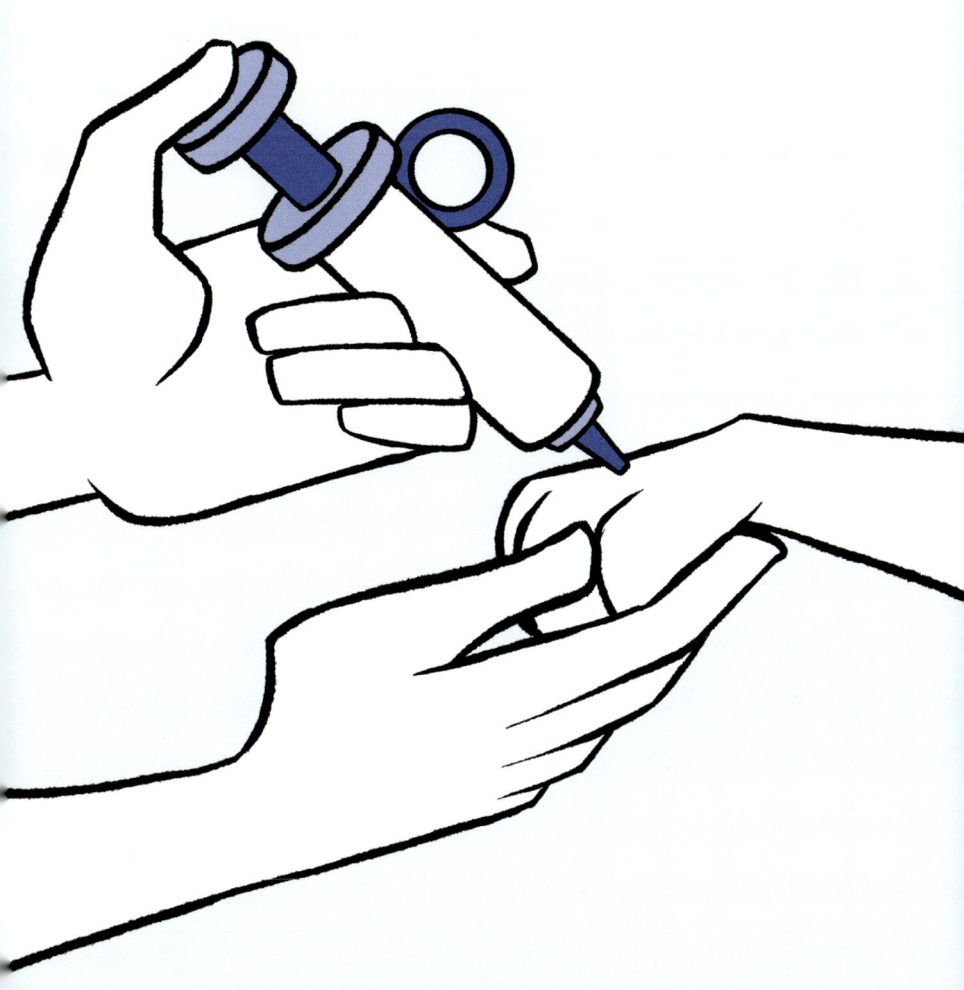

Maddie takes a deep breath and looks at Rita. "Okay, I'm ready. Can Cricket sit by me?"

I look to Tunde. "Cricket would like that too!" he smiles. Tunde places me next to Maddie's left arm while she holds her right arm out to Rita.

I rest my chin on Maddie's left arm to help her stay calm and still. Rita inserts the IV with only a slight flinch from Maddie. *She did it!*

"Good job, Maddie!" Tunde claps. "I saw you hold your body still like a statue and take slow, deep breaths."

Maddie's tense muscles relax. She wraps her free arm around my neck. "Thanks for your help, Cricket."

Tunde nods to me as he commands, "Shake." I hold up my paw. Maddie takes it into her hand and squeezes.

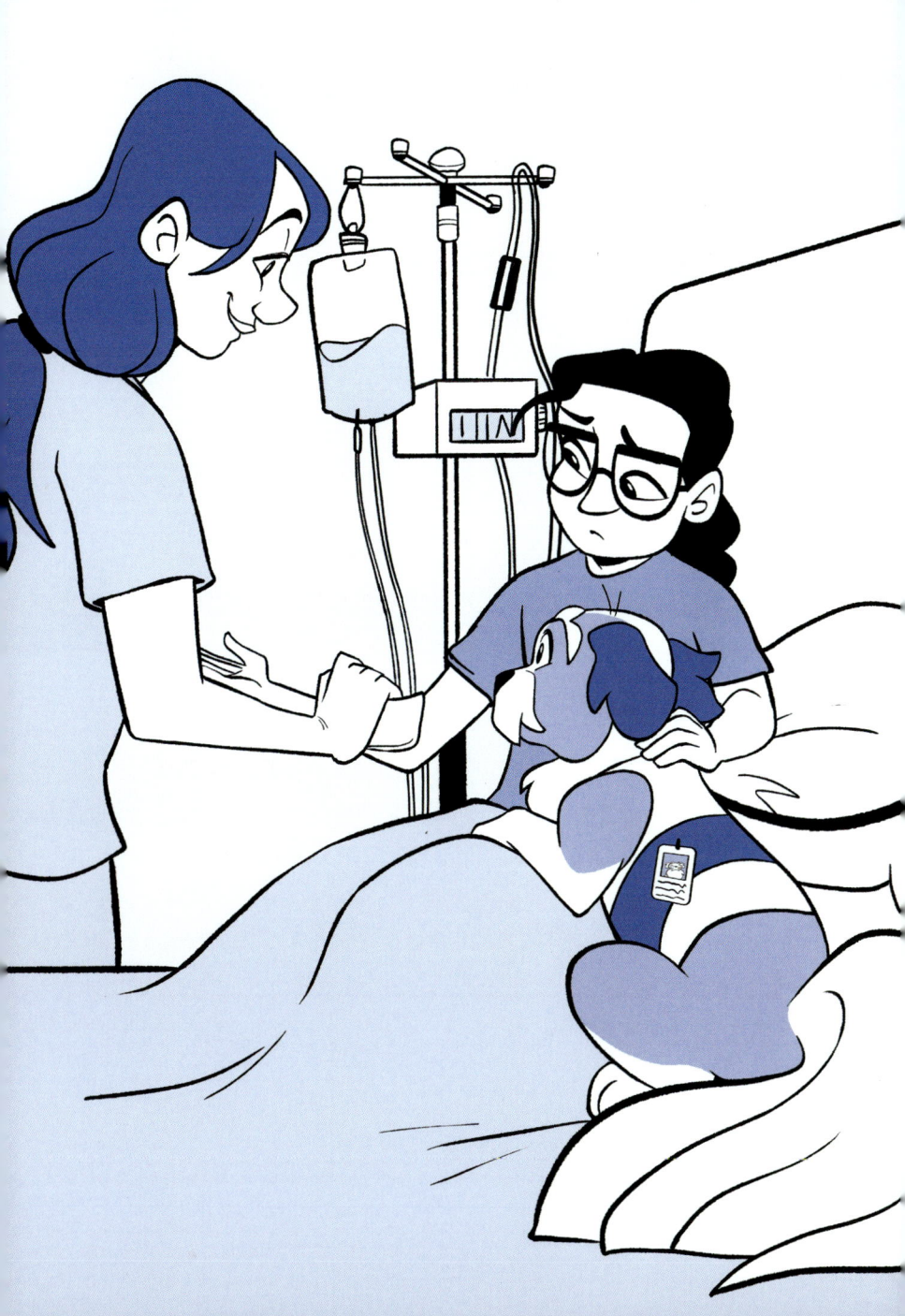

"You're going to do great, Maddie," Tunde assures her.

Rita opens the door and rolls in a different bed. "It's time for surgery, Maddie. We're going to transfer you onto this bed. Dr. Zinnecker will take excellent care of you, and you'll be done in no time."

Maddie's parents hug and kiss her. I nuzzle my nose into her neck before I jump off her bed.

"Bye, Cricket," Maddie says with a wave. "I'll see you later."

I wag my tail as she's rolled down the hallway. I still haven't found Maddie's smile, but I will.

SAM NEEDS A SCAN

BACK IN THE HALL, TUNDE KNEELS AND SCRUBS MY EARS with both hands.

"Cricket, you were a big help to Maddie," he says. "Good job, girl." He scratches my chin before standing. "How about we take a break and then check on some other patients while we wait for Maddie to get out of surgery?"

I bounce on my front paws. Tunde usually takes me to the park near the hospital for break time.

"Want to visit the ducks at the park?" he says, reading my mind.

Yes! I sit up straight to show Tunde I'm interested. His deep laughter fills the hospital corridor.

"Okay, let's go."

Tunde whistles as we walk down the street to the park. He stops twice on the sidewalk to chat with other hospital staff. I want to tug on my leash to keep him moving, but my training taught me to be patient. It sure is hard sometimes!

Kids hang from monkey bars and zip down the slide at the park playground. Singing and laughter fill the air. Tunde

and I walk around the park, pausing every now and then so I can sniff flowers and bushes.

As we near the duck pond, I spot Lumos and Eun Ji walking toward us on the path. Tunde waves to Eun Ji. While they chat, I proudly tell Lumos about my morning.

"I was in the emergency room, where I helped Maddie get an IV before surgery. She has appendicitis!"

Lumos's ears perk up. "That sounds stressful, Cricket. Good work!"

"I hope she feels better after her appendectomy. Her belly was really hurting."

Lumos tilts his head to the side. "She'll be sore after surgery, but it will be a different pain. She'll be happy to see you when she wakes up."

"Thanks, Lumos. I'll keep her comfortable. How is your day going?"

Lumos reflects for a moment before responding. "It's been eventful. Sydney is a patient in rehab. She walked me down the hall today and made it farther than she's ever walked!"

"That's great news, Lumos!"

"Yes, Sydney was fantastic!" Lumos looks down. "But as soon as we returned to her room, she received bad news. Her cat ran away."

"Oh, no," I say, though I don't quite understand why Lumos is upset. In my experience, cats are moody and unpleasant.

"Sydney was so sad," Lumos continues.

"I couldn't do anything to make her smile. Usually, I'm pretty good at that."

"Lumos, you're the best facility dog I know," I assure him. "You helped Sydney walk again! She probably just needed some time alone."

Lumos looks into my eyes. "Thanks, Cricket. I needed that."

Tunde tugs on my leash. "Let's go, Cricket. Break time's over. Back to work!"

I feel refreshed as we walk back into the hospital. Tunde takes his patient list out of his pocket and looks at his watch.

"We're just in time for Sam's CT scan. Let's catch him at radiology." Tunde hurries down the corridor, and I trot alongside him.

Tunde explains that ten-year-old Sam has had leg surgery, and the bone isn't healing well. He needs a special X-ray called a CT scan every week, and he doesn't like it one bit.

The radiology department is where they take X-rays and other special images. The exam rooms hold amazing machines that can see inside the body! Tunde stops outside a room with a sign that reads "Computerized Tomography." He opens the door and peeks his head inside.

"Hey, Mary. Are we on time for Sam's CT scan?"

Mary opens the door wide. "Hey, Tunde. Hi, Cricket. Sam just arrived. Let's go chat with him."

A young boy sits in a wheelchair with a blanket wrapped around his shoulders. His left leg is in a cast up to his hip. He looks frustrated.

"Sam, this is Tunde," Mary says. "And this is Cricket. They came to help you with your CT scan today."

Sam grumbles. "I'm so tired of these scans."

"I bet you're sick of hospitals and wheelchairs, too," Tunde says. "I don't blame you for being frustrated."

Tunde lifts me up so Sam can scratch my head. Sam and I lock eyes. "Hi, there," he says quietly.

"Do you mind if Cricket shows you how she gets a CT scan?" Tunde asks Sam.

Sam looks at me, then up at Tunde. His eyes light up. "She can do that?"

"Of course she can!" Tunde says as he places me on the long, narrow bed of the CT scanner. "Roll, Cricket."

I flop onto my back and stick my paws into the air. *It's pretty relaxing here.*

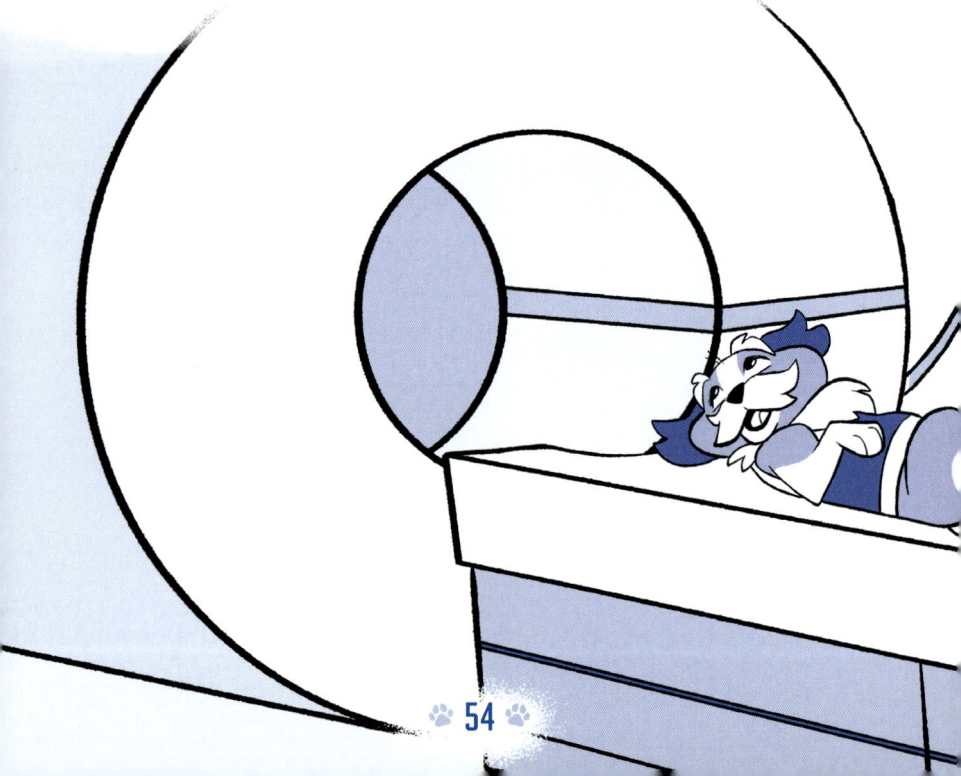

Tunde turns to Sam. "See how Cricket relaxes? The key is to think happy thoughts and let your body go soft. I wonder what Cricket's thinking about?"

Frisbee, kibble, Ralph the moose, Frisbee...

Mary's voice chimes over a speaker from the control room. "Remember to hold very still, Cricket."

The table moves, and the bed slides inside a big circle. It's like I'm riding on a sled! I stay still and relaxed.

Sam looks at the machine and shakes his head. "I just don't like it."

Tunde nods his head. "I know it might feel scary sometimes. Next time think of

Cricket, paws in the air and dreaming of playing Frisbee."

I grin to myself. *How did he know?*

Sam laughs. "I'm going to think about Frisbee too."

As Tunde lifts me off the bed, Mary steps into the room. "You ready, Sam?" she asks.

"I'm ready," Sam says, giving me one last scratch behind my ears.

Tunde pats Sam on the shoulder and gives him a wink. "You got this, Sam. Just keep your eye on the Frisbee."

REST & RECOVERY

TUNDE AND I HEAD TO THE MEDICAL FLOOR SO WE'LL be there when Maddie comes back from surgery. I wait on Tunde's lap, my ears perked for the slightest sound in the hallway. I hope everything went well!

Tunde and I stand when a nurse rolls Maddie's bed into the room.

The nurse introduces herself to Mr. and Mrs. Tan. "I'm Cindy, and I'll be Maddie's nurse until she's ready to leave the hospital."

Lying on the bed, Maddie looks different. She has a clear tube in her nose, and her eyes are closed. *Is she okay?* I look at Tunde and sit close to his leg.

"Maddie's okay," Tunde tells me. "She's still asleep from anesthesia, but she'll wake up soon."

I wag my tail to tell Tunde I'm relieved.

Maddie stirs in her bed and pulls at the tube in her nose.

Cindy speaks softly. "It's okay, Maddie. That tube's job is to give your body extra air to breathe. We can take it out now that you're waking up." Cindy gently removes the tube from Maddie's nose.

Mr. and Mrs. Tan move in on either side of Maddie as her eyes open. "Hey, sweetheart! You're all done."

Maddie shifts in her bed and blinks her eyes. She looks confused.

Tunde steps in. "Maddie's still waking up from anesthesia. Sometimes people get a little anxious and confused." He looks at Maddie's parents. "Would you mind if Cricket snuggled next to her? That can provide comfort."

Mr. and Mrs. Tan nod their heads and smile. Tunde places me next to Maddie's arm, and her hand finds my fur. She pulls me close and mumbles, "Cricket?"

I lie still and let her scratch my back. I'm so happy she's awake.

Cindy hooks up tubes to Maddie's IV. "I'm going to give her a little pain medicine. She might feel uncomfortable, but Dr. Zinnecker says the surgery went well. She'll be out of here in no time."

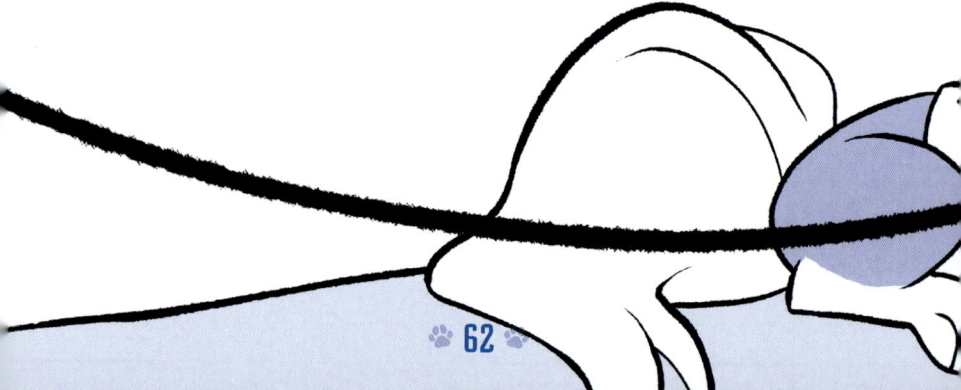

Maddie's eyes flutter open. "Then I get to go home?"

Cindy smiles as she gives my head a scratch. "When you're able to eat and take some walks, then you'll be able to go home."

My ears perk up. I can help Maddie with those things! But for right now, I'll rest by her side for a nice nap.

I wake up to belly rubs and my feet pointing toward the ceiling. *How long have I been asleep?*

Maddie is awake and talking to her mom and dad. She sounds sad. "Why does my belly still hurt?" she asks.

"Your belly needs time to heal," Tunde answers. "The sick appendix is gone, but now you'll have discomfort from the surgery. Do you want to see your tummy?"

Maddie nods, and I sit up beside her. Cindy lifts Maddie's gown to show three tiny bandages on her stomach.

Mr. Tan leans in. "That's it?" he asks. "How did they get her appendix out of those tiny incisions?"

Tunde bellows his deep laugh. "Surgeons can do amazing things!"

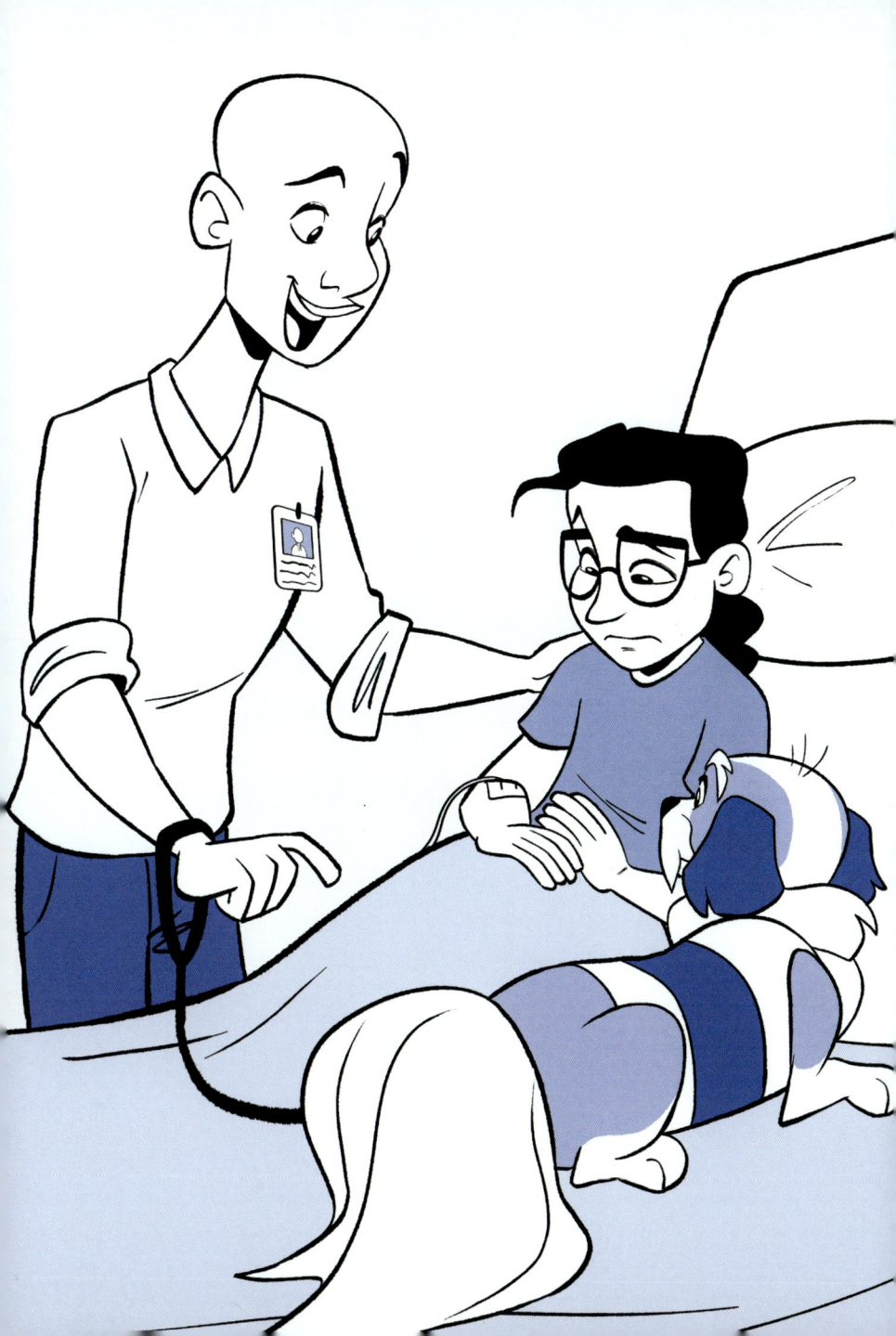

"What do you think about sitting on the edge of the bed for a while, Maddie?" Cindy asks.

Maddie nods. I move aside as she slowly swings her legs over the edge of the bed. Her cheeks are pink. She looks much better than when I first saw her. After more rest and some delicious-looking Jell-O, Maddie can stand beside her bed without feeling wobbly.

"How about we take a walk?" Tunde holds one of my leashes and hands a second one to Maddie.

Maddie's eyes light up. "I get to walk Cricket?"

I look up at Tunde with wide eyes. "I think Cricket would love it!" Tunde laughs.

As we walk down the hallway, Maddie shuffles her feet at first. But soon she gains confidence, and her strides grow stronger. I prance with my head and tail held high. I'm so proud of her! When it's time for Tunde and me to leave, Maddie pulls me into a big hug. "Thanks, Cricket."

I happy-pant and place my paw on her arm. Then I see what I'd been looking for all day: Maddie's smile.

I knew I'd find it!

THE LUCKIEST PUP

AFTER LEAVING MADDIE'S ROOM, MY FEET FLOAT DOWN the hallway. I'm so relieved she's feeling better!

Tunde squats down and rubs behind my ears. "You did excellent today, Cricket. Good girl."

While Tunde packs up for the day, Lumos and Eun Ji stop to say goodbye. They're leaving for the day too.

"Cricket, you were right," Lumos says. "I got to see Sydney this afternoon.

She was still upset about her cat, but she wanted to go on another walk."

"I told you, Lumos. You're the best facility dog around!"

Lumos grins wide. "You're not so bad yourself! Maddie was lucky to have you."

Aw, shucks! I feel my cheeks flush and my stomach flutter.

This might just be the best day *ever*.

Tunde drives us home as soft jazz plays on the radio. He doesn't say much, and I can see in his eyes that he's tired too.

When we get home, Tunde makes dinner while he whistles a happy tune. "I'm making you a special dish tonight, Cricket, for your good work with Maddie."

Tunde sets down my food bowl. He's arranged my kibble into the shape of a heart. *I love you too, Tunde!* I devour every bite and lick my bowl clean.

Ralph the moose waits in my bed. I grab him by his antler and snuggle up with Tunde on the couch. Tunde turns on a movie, and I feel my eyes grow heavy.

If not for Helping Paws Academy, I wouldn't be here with Tunde. And I wouldn't have met Maddie! I rest my head on Ralph's and close my eyes. *I'm the luckiest pup around.*

A Note from Maddie:
MORE ABOUT APPENDICITIS

HI READER, IT'S MADDIE HERE! CRICKET AND TUNDE helped me learn so much about appendicitis. I feel great after my surgery and want to share what I've learned.

The appendix is a small pouch that comes out of the large intestine. When the appendix becomes infected and inflamed, it's called appendicitis. This causes bacteria to grow and multiply, forming pus. If the infected appendix is not removed, it can rupture, or burst. This causes bacteria to spread into the belly.

When I had appendicitis, my symptoms came on quickly. The pain started around my belly button, then moved to my lower right belly. The pain got worse when I moved or coughed. People with appendicitis may also experience nausea, low appetite, and bloating. Anyone with these symptoms should contact a doctor immediately!

Doctors like mine diagnose appendicitis with blood tests. They also use CT scans or ultrasounds to see images of the appendix. My CT scan showed a swollen appendix. That's why I needed a surgeon to remove it in a procedure called an appendectomy. It sounded scary at first, but I was given medicine called anesthesia to make sure I was asleep for the whole thing. Now I'm back to my usual smiling self!

A Note from Cricket:
MORE ABOUT FACILITY DOGS

HELLO, FRIEND! CRICKET HERE. SINCE BECOMING a facility dog, I've told all my two- and four-legged pals about it. I'd love to tell you too!

Facility dogs like me are specially trained to work at a certain facility, such as a hospital or other healthcare setting, where we offer physical and emotional support to adults and children. We respond to more than forty commands to motivate patients and help them work toward their goals. Facility dogs are considered full-time workers, and their handlers are facility employees.

If you'd like to learn more about facility dogs, check out the websites below. And hey, thanks for reading!

Canine Companions—What Are the Differences Between Service Dogs, Facility Dogs, Therapy Dogs and Emotional Support Animals?

https://canine.org/service-dogs/service-dog-month/service-dog-differences/

Pet Partners—Terminology

https://petpartners.org/learn/terminology/

MEET ALICIA!

ALICIA IS THE FACILITY DOG AT MAYO CLINIC Children's Center. The Golden Labrador was expertly trained from birth to two years old at Canine Companions. She works directly with her handler, Amy, CCLS, and their patient population.

Together, Amy and Alicia support patients' physical and psychological needs throughout their hospital stays. Alicia provides comfort during non-sterile procedures and motivation during treatment and recovery. She also takes part in medical play to help young patients understand and cooperate with their treatments or procedures.

At Mayo Clinic Children's Center, pediatric experts diagnose and treat all types of diseases and disorders in children. Specialists from different areas work as a team to find answers, set goals, and develop a treatment plan tailored to every child's needs.

READ ALL THE BOOKS IN THE HELPING PAWS ACADEMY SERIES!

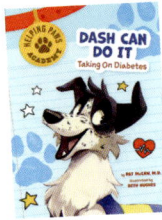

PAT McCAW, M.D., IS A FAMILY PRACTICE PHYSICIAN AND CHILDREN'S AUTHOR from Eldridge, Iowa. She is passionate about using books to help children with emotional and health issues. In addition to writing, she practices family medicine part-time and is a faculty physician at a medical residency program. Pat teaches classes on how to use picture books in the classroom and writes online educational lessons on science and physiology. If she has any free time, she loves to hike and fish while spending time with her family. Her dog, Poppy, rules the household. Pat's website and blog is found at www.patmccawauthor.com.